D0910110

DISCARDED
From Nashville Public Library

THE ORIGIN OF THE WORLD

Books by Pierre Michon

in English
Masters and Servants

in French
Vies minuscules
Vie de Joseph Roulin
L'Empereur d'Occident
Maîtres et serviteurs
Rimbaud le fils
La Grande Beune
Le Rois du bois
Trois auteurs
Mythologies d'hiver

THE ORIGIN OF THE WORLD BY PIERRE MICHON
TRANSLATED FROM THE FRENCH BY WYATT ALEXANDER MASON

MERCURY HOUSE
San Francisco

Originally published as *La Grande Beune* ©1996 Éditions Verdier, France.
Translation copyright ©2002 by Wyatt Alexander Mason.

A note on the title: Michon's working title was *L'Origine du monde*. Shortly prior
to publication, however, another work came out so named, thus he chose *La
Grande Beune*. For the American edition, the author prefers that his original title be
preserved.

Published in the United States by Mercury House, San Francisco, California, a
nonprofit publishing company devoted to the free exchange of ideas and guided
by a dedication to literary values. Mercury House and colophon are registered
trademarks of Mercury House, Inc. Visit us at: http://www.mercuryhouse.org.

This work, published as part of a program of aid for publication, received support
from the French Ministry of Foreign Affairs and the Cultural Services of the
French Embassy in the United States. *Cet ouvrage, publié dans le cadre d'un pro-
gramme, d'aide à la publication bénéficie du soutien du Ministère des Affaires
étrangères et du Service Culturel de l'Ambassade de France aux États-Unis.*

Printed on acid-free paper and manufactured by Sheridan Books, Chelsea, MI.

Cover art: "Untitled" by Robert Longo; courtesy of the artist.
Book design by Mark Barry of sübata
Proofread by Laura Harger

Library of Congress Cataloguing in Publication Data:
Michon, Pierre, 1945–
    [Grande Beune. English]
    The origin of the world / by Pierre Michon ; translated from the French by
Wyatt Alexander Mason.
        p. cm.
    ISBN 1-56279-126-5 (hardcover : alk. paper)
    I. Mason, Wyatt Alexander, 1969– . II. Title.
    PQ2673.1298G7314 2002
    843'.914—dc21

        2002025541

THE ORIGIN OF THE WORLD

The Earth slept naked and tormented like
a mother whose bedcovers have slipped away.

Andrei Platanov

ONE

Between les Martres and Saint-Amand-le-Petit lies the town of Castelnau, along the Beune. I was posted to Castelnau in 1961: devils are posted as well I suppose, to their Circles below; and somersault after somersault make their downward way just as we slip gently toward retirement. I hadn't fallen yet, not exactly, it was my first post, I was twenty. There's no train station in Castelnau; it's long gone; buses leaving Brive or Périgueux early in the morning drop you there at the end of the line very late at night. I arrived at night, in something close to shock, in the middle of a galloping September rain that bucked in the beams of the headlights, in the pounding of the long windshield wipers; I couldn't see the village at all, the rain was black. I took a room *Chez Hélène,* Castelnau's only hotel, perched on the lip of the cliff beneath which the Beune flows: that night, I couldn't yet see the Beune, but leaning out the window of my room, I was just able to make out a hollow in the darkness behind the hotel.

Three steps took you down into the bar; it was painted that blood red once called *rouge antique;* it smelled of saltpeter; between long silences, a scattering of seated drinkers spoke loudly of gunshots and fishing; their movements in the low light cast their shadows over the walls; if you looked above the counter you would see a stuffed fox staring out at you, its pointy head turned violently your way but its body running along the length of the wall, as if in flight. The night, the creature's eyes, the red walls, these people's rough talk, their archaic words —all of this sent me back to some uncertain, pleasureless moment past, filled me with a vague fear that was compounded by the fear of soon having to face my students: this past seemed to be my future, these shady fishermen whose captains were loading me onto the rickety raft of adult life and who, reaching the river's middle, were stripping me and throwing me to the bottom, snickering in the darkness, in their beards, in their bad patois; later, they would squat along the banks and wordlessly scale enormous fish. September's bewildered rain was beating the windows. Hélène was as old and massive as the Cumaean sibyl, as pensive, but all dolled up in nice old clothes, her hair in a scarf; her fat arm and its uprolled sleeve wiped the table in front of me; her least movement radiated pride, a silent joy: I wondered how she'd come to run this red tavern presided over by a fox. I asked her for some dinner; she apologized modestly, for her ovens that had gone cold for the night, for her advanced years, and then served me a profusion of cold morsels that pilgrims and soldiers in stories are forever filling up on before their bodies are run through with swords, as they cross a black ford full of blades. And wine, in a fat glass, to better brave these blades. I ate these haute-époque cold cuts; at the neighboring table words came infrequently; heads drew nearer, heavied with sleep or the memory of animals about to pounce, dying; these were young men; but their fatigue, their hunts, these were as old as fables. My Wallachian brigands at last donned their hats, stood, and in their inky black oilcoats whose broken folds gleamed moved off bravely to perform the strange orders of boatmen, of the sleeping world; one of them, above his starry greatcoat, had turned his finely featured face toward me; he offered a complicitous smile, or perhaps it was only pity; either way, his teeth shined a bright white. You could hear the mopeds starting up. Through the open door, the night was turbid, moveless: the rain was galloping elsewhere; there was fog. "It's Jean the Fisherman," Hélène said, with a little nod of her head toward this fog through which the shrill motors flew; her gesture was so vague that she could just as easily have been naming the fog. She smiled. The wrinkles in this smile sorted themselves out perfectly. She shut the door, fiddled with some switches, the lights went out; rising, I was already asleep; I was anywhere, in lands where foxes run through dreams, in the heart of a fog of fish one doesn't see leap from the water, falling back in with a hard flat noise, at the very bottom of Dordogne, which is to say nowhere, in Wallachia.

It rained all of September.

My students weren't monsters: they were children who were afraid of everything and laughed for no reason. They had given me the little class, not the smallest but the elementary level; it was composed of many little bodies that all looked alike; I learned how to name them, to recognize them during recess as they ran through the rain to the windy hollow beneath the covered playground; I would observe them from behind the high windows of the room, and then all of a sudden I wouldn't see them anymore; they would be huddled under an awning, beneath the blithe bodies of falling rain. I was alone in the classroom. I looked at a long row of pegs from which their car coats hung, still steaming from the morning rain as if drying in some bivouac, the belongings of a dwarf army; I named even these little castoffs, said them aloud with some emotion. And of course there were big blackboards on the walls bearing letters and syllables, words and phrases flanked by drawings, posters, all the predictable imagery, the naïve nothings that charm young hearts, hook them, while flogging them with times tables that make them cry beneath these innocuous lures, pictures of plump little boys laughing, of young girls with braids, of rabbits. Children move their feet when they think, when they cry: I could see the traces of this careful, sad dance beneath their desks, little circles of mud; and large inkblots on the white wood testified to the same rhythm, to the same piety. Yes, this moved me; I wasn't much older than they, I was twenty; and I was drifting away, I was barely even there.

What slept beneath the dust in a glass display case in the rear of the class came from a deeper beyond. The case was from the last century, from the era of socialist savants, of the three Jules, of yet another Republic, from a time when athletic curates of the Périgord would roll up their cassocks and crawl through caves in search of Adam's remains, a time when instructors, from Périgord as well, were themselves crawling around in the mud with a couple of brats in tow, making their way to remains that would prove once and for all that man wasn't born of Adam; such was the provenance of the case's contents, as the labels affixed to each object attested, learned names calligraphied in a fine hand typical of the time, a beautiful hand, vain, rounded, cluttered, ardent, a hand they all shared, the fools, each group more modest than the next, those who believed in Scripture and those who believed in mankind's glorious tomorrows; but the case held artifacts from our century as well, however stingy by comparison; how the calligraphy had suffered at Verdun, how the calligraphy had fallen to ashes, to spidery scrawls, in the hells of Poland and Slovakia, in infamous camps not far from Attila's own but which made Attila's look like schools of philosophy, fields of beets and watch-towers that neither God nor man would have use of again; and despite Verdun and the Slovakian fog, the teachers, without this fine hand, had continued all the same, heroically in a sense, to put long names on little stones, with the faith that remained theirs, that of habit, which was better than nothing; and beyond just arriving from teachers of every stripe, the contents were gathered by other men as well, men who had made things, not just labels, men of whom we can no longer say whether they believed in something while making them or whether they believed in nothing and made them out of habit, but whom we rightly believe never demeaned themselves as deeply as those in the Slovakian Circles. These were just stones. What one calls weapons; harpoons, battle-axes, blades, though they seemed like stones that the ground spits up after rainstorms, which they were as well; these were flints, the fabulous silicates that had received the names of long-forgotten villages and which in return had saddled these villages with the weight of history, had burrowed underneath an infinity of catacombs, older than Mycenae, older than Memphis, than Genesis with all its dead, and so convincingly that we ask ourselves to whom the Mayor of Les Eyzies was addressing himself on the eleventh of November, with his little piece of paper wavering in the north wind, standing before a monument to the dead; these crude flints, precious in their own way like the gold coffins in the Valley of the Kings; more precious; the noble flints with royal patronyms drawn from their parishes in Somme, in Lot, in Yonne, and which too carry first names of fishes and trees, of birds—*Willow Leaf of Solutré, Parrot's Beak of Madeleine, Great Dab of Saint-Acheul*—but which quickly acquired sobriquets—*the loveliest, the oldest, the most perverse*—each a shimmering jewel, and each of which nonetheless could kill a cow, impeccably. The display case sat there: we were right around the corner from Lascaux, the Beune flows into the old Vézère valley, the ground brims with these implements of slaughter, these obsolete grenades forever with pins pulled and bouncing through brooks, freezing in the ice, rising through the roots of fallen trees and leaping from ditches upturned by the plow, children collecting them on a road and carrying them to school under their bonnets, in their little Wallachian hats, and with a sweet smile offering them to a teacher well versed in such things, interested in them, held in their weak little hands, these bits of darkness. That accomplished, they sit, slip off their schoolbags, and unwind by shuffling their feet, tipping their braids and necks over pages where little rabbits show them how to read; and to make their parents happy, their teacher, and even they themselves occasionally, they try to grow up unfazed by what looms behind them, in a display case filled with stickers. These stones rolled all the way to the Castelnau school and were waiting for the flood that would roll them elsewhere, remaining stickered this time so that they might be read by fish. There was another quarter hour to kill before the end of recess; through the window there was still this rain, this fog filled with people that Hélène called Jean the Fisherman; two little bundles below were attempting an outing in the courtyard, moving at a gallop, running with shivery, excited cries back to the playground; I left the stones there, their low weights; I was sitting on my desk; I was listening to their legs. I was giving myself over to another devotion, to another brand of violence. I was thinking about the tobacconist.

The Tabac was beneath the old arcade, on the fairground that is Castelnau's square, home to its businesses. I went in shortly after my arrival, after school, of an evening. And of course it was raining, my hair was soaking wet; the shop was empty. I looked vaguely at the revolving postcard stand by the door, saw the abandoned wolf of Font-de-Gaume and the great cows of Lascaux, the round bison, and the outrageous women from the same era that they call Venuses, their outsized asses, their long fine necks. Pictures like this are sold throughout the region. In this zoo, this harem, a strange image stopped me for a moment: it was a reproduction of a shoddily painted plaster statuette, a monk in his frock collapsed against the stump of a tree, to which he's nailed here and there by long arrows; his tonsured head is askew; the man is dead. Putting the card back, I read that this was the blessed Jean-Gabriel Perboyre, a Jesuit whom the Chinese tortured to death around 1650, a native of Castelnau. Although it was all a bit much, the tilt of his head nonetheless screamed loss, made it moving, a sort of resignation, perhaps even despair, which didn't quite look right on a saint, given he was dead. I heard the hit of her heels; I turned around and she was behind her counter. I saw her from the waist up. Her arms were bare.

Women of rare and subtle beauty have never really

done it for me, beauties that slowly reveal themselves with time; I want them to suddenly manifest out of the ether like ghosts. And this one had me pondering abominable thoughts instantly, thoughts that ran through my blood. Saying she was a nice piece is saying nothing at all. She was tall and white, a white like milk. She was grand and ripe like the houri Above, unbridled but reined in, cinched tightly at her waist; if animals stare almost bodily, she was an animal; if queens carry themselves as if with their heads atop columns, upright and pure, clement but lethal, she was a queen. Her royal face was as bare as a belly: and within this face, beneath raven hair, were such pale eyes, eyes forever the miraculous preserve of the fair, a secret light beneath darkness that if by some miracle you might have such a woman would nonetheless remain an enigma that nothing, neither lifted dresses nor heightened voices, can ever lay bare. She was somewhere between thirty and forty years old. Everything about her screamed desire, something that people say enough that it's almost meaningless, but it was a quality that she gave of generously to everyone, to herself, to nothing, when she was alone and had forgotten herself, setting something in motion while settling a fingertip to the counter, turning her head slightly, gold earrings brushing her cheek while she watched you or watched nothing at all; this desire was open, like a wound; and she knew it, wore it with valor, with passion. But what are words? She wasn't clay: more the beating of wings in a storm, and yet no flesh could conceivably have been more perfectly ample, more substantial, more bound by its weight. The weight of this torso, so slender despite the blossoming of her breasts, was considerable. Packages of cigarettes haloed her in neat rows. I couldn't see her skirt; it was nonetheless there, behind the counter, vast, unliftable. Outside, hard rain lashed the windows: I could hear it crackle on this unsullied flesh.

My hair was still dripping on my forehead. This woman, her lips lightly parted, benevolent and mildly surprised, patiently considered my silence. She was waiting to hear what I wanted. I spoke in a dream, in a voice nonetheless clear. She turned around, her armpit appearing when she lifted her arm to the shelves, and her hand, smooth and beringed, opened under my eyes with a red-and-white box of Marlboros in its palm. I brushed it while taking the box. Perhaps to see this gesture again—the coins resting in her palm, painted nails joining and separating—I also bought the postcard of the arrowed saint. She smiled, broadly. "Would you like an envelope?" she said. Absolutely I did. Her voice was generous as well, words like gifts. Once more the white arm plunged, her fingers joined, her earrings caressed her cheek. When I left, the sky was just beginning to clear; the cobbles shone, rejuvenated; the rain had ended. Along the slope toward the auberge, toward the Beune, the sun appeared, the sky opening and the pale trees appearing indelibly against the sky; in my throat, in my ears, something plaintive remained, something powerful, like an unending cry cut short, modulating, full of tears and invincible desire, a desire that rises from nocturnal throats, cinched tight but strangely free, like the word *honey* in a blues tune. In the bar chez Hélène, the sun could be seen setting over the Beune, dark black clouds bending over like maidservants, approaching; love that moves stars stirred the stars, dolled them up, made them look like Esthers, stripped them bare to white, instantly; sunlight caressed the red fur of the fox, little children in the countryside saw a rain-dipped pebble and it would be in a fist they would offer me tomorrow with something like love; up above, on the square, the tobacconist was already shivering from the brutal festivities of the night to come, her hand perhaps trembling briefly on a packet of Marlboros, her skirt caressing her thighs. *Honey:* when the sun goes down, when night comes, when the souls of women are as naked as their hands.

Did I dare think she could be mine? Of course, and

feverishly, but only by some miracle, no more shocking after all than the miracle by which she existed in Castelnau, and that from her divine hand she could birth packets of Marlboros. I was of an age when one believed that one had nothing to offer, nothing one could exchange against such wealth, such thighs and breasts, gold earrings and the call from her skirts, nothing, and especially not that incongruous thing that grows magnificently from our groin. And what's more, I was of that ridiculous generation embarrassed by everything, that imagined a woman's desire was subject to one's ability to talk about notable, serious matters, pop songs or paintings, politics, some blob of nothing; or, if you can't talk to them, at least make sure that they think you can. And I was a good-looking kid, charming enough, and I had enough in my pants to convince her—or would have, it will soon be clear, had she not already belonged to another, as they say. So I didn't try a thing, I made no more move for her hand than to collect the little red-and-white boxes; and I added a dash of loftiness to the part by buying *Le Monde* every day, which I didn't read—she also sold newspapers—the copies of which piled up in my room above the great tangled hole of the Beune, and of course she didn't witness anything in my actions that would have won me any points, she couldn't have cared less. I went to the shop every day, out of my real passion for tobacco and my feigned passion for undigested newsprint, which were justification enough: we exchanged a few words, she always offered her smile and the warmth of her voice, she was patient, her skirt rustled, occasionally I saw her legs, and her heels, always high.

TWO

I had noticed that often, on Sundays and certain afternoons, she went by foot along la route des Martres, always in high heels no matter what weather, all dolled up, returning much later or not at all—unless she had come back via a shortcut I didn't know. I didn't need to ask what she was doing there: the sky was my answer, to see her beneath it was enough. This road soon became my passion. There were great meadows, and dark walnut trees at the edge of the village, and farther along were woods crisscrossed by footpaths leading to various hamlets; the road followed the lip of the cliff, sometimes climbing steeply, with hiding places lost behind masses of fallen rock, hollows in the sides of hills from which one could only see sky, secret resting places beneath beeches. There, on my free afternoons, most often beneath the rain, I pretended to get some air and to take a profound interest in plants and pebbles—instructors are allowed their eccentricities—but of course I was pacing the paths and was waiting, tensed, consumed by a painful image that flowed through me, her image, as if she were in my blood, images of a woman in her Sunday best, then naked and dressed again and naked again, a rhythm of stockings, of gold and of skin, a thousand silks beating this silken flesh. With such thoughts I made my way to the Beune; I watched it flow through its hole down below, dirty waters beneath a dirty sky in which unseen fish were spawning, eyes wide open and doleful: and yet this world was beautiful nonetheless, if stockings could fill my soul, could strip it bare while I stripped imaginary flesh. I returned beneath the shelter of the trees. I stopped suddenly; I imagined her mouth; I imagined her neck; at the thought of the rest of her I trembled with a feeling well beyond desire. At the sight of you, I told myself, perhaps she will wordlessly let her head fall back, will tremble as you tremble, will seize you where you want to seize her, and with her skirts in her hands she will give herself over, against this birch, in these puddles into which her earrings will have fallen, where she will paw the ground, where you will see her breasts, and, more shaken than a tree in the wind, her great tumbling cries will scare the crows away. I heard a sound, my heart collapsed. I resumed the bearing of an attentive botanist; it was nothing, a spooked animal: but other times she was there, in the foliage, the mud, with her high heels and her perfect makeup, all of her, sometimes in gloves, her hands in the pockets of her raincoat, her head high, a queen, stopping near me, talking about the bad weather, sweetly telling me that I smoked too much; I responded from the same script, I fell into her smile, I wanted to hold onto this drop of rain clutched in the down of her cheek, hesitating, flowing. The pale violet rings beneath her eyes tore at me, her perfume in the woods pressed into my stomach. She moved off, her skirts rustling louder than the trees, her heels piercing fallen leaves. Her hands were in her pockets. The raincoat flared out around her hips. I was suffocating. The world was white flesh, a nice piece at that. The arrows that pierced and burned Jean-Gabriel Perboyre collapsed on his tree stump burned no more than those that pierced me, collapsed upon my own, receiving pleasure from hands no longer my own, but hers: the delights that she filled me with, that, in a way, she gave me herself, because I'm certain that she wasn't unaware of them, are the most pointed I have ever felt. Sometimes she wasn't there at all.

I would return only near nightfall. Through the walnuts my Wallachian village loomed up above, the school perched there since the three Jules reigned, the drowsing arsenal, the panoply of old men who had felt desire in the woods; and the church below with its little Jean-Gabriel within who had wished to be tortured on the Yellow River, had been so and had so been thankful; and the eternal auberge. The branches and the rain threw themselves at the windowpane. A kettle was singing, the percolator was smoking. I was soaked through but was boiling in all this wet. I sat down dumbfounded beneath the familiar fox; there were a few drinkers in smoldering oilskins, boatmen taking long draws on their beers as if stuck to the counter and yet seemingly transported to some other side, another bank that looks just like this one, where there are the same people, but that is softer, hotter, more alive; Jean the Fisherman wasn't with them—he didn't live there and he didn't come by every night—I'd seen him leave before dawn to catch eel or who knows what, he'd winked while turning away and had disappeared with his hoop nets, his spider over his shoulder, toward the Little Beune. Hélène served me more of her endless ham, her musketeers' pâtés; my desire hadn't waned, it weighed on my stomach while I ate. My thoughts roamed the landscape, I was drifting away. In this blood red room that smelled of cigarette butts, of rotten wine casks, of saltpeter, I was imagining that all the drinkers were making for the black, for night, toward what they couldn't resist, the tobacconist giving herself over to this call, sitting up in her bed, throwing her raincoat over her shoulders and rushing to the auberge, twisting her ankles on her high heels, this queen, coming in like the wind, opening her raincoat with two trembling hands, throwing herself naked onto one of the sticky tables, onto the silent pinball machine, shedding her earrings, her eyes white with ecstasy, all for my unique use, beneath Hélène's thoughtful eye, behind her counter, watching Yvonne move through every position, knowing her raven hair, her orgeat thighs, her mother-of-pearl ass, all shining immoderately beneath a fox, her cries tumbling out like an eagle's, hurtling over the cliff, startling poachers crouched along the Beune. I gutted her.

Hélène cleared the tables, deep in thought, her heavy arm wiping gracefully. I wondered what once had been beneath her fine old rags: it didn't seem to bother her that there was no longer anything there, she had shaken off that finer flesh, that want that throws even the youngest hearts toward drama and night, both debases and blesses, felling them to all fours where they lose themselves in pleasure, and still on all fours and barely less frenzied are other times lost in pain, in grief, in misery. Hélène's dead flesh was radiant. Her flesh was no longer hers but was elsewhere, detached, free of her, fishing eels over the Little Beune, resting on her elbows in another bistro in Saint-Amand-le-Petit, amazing the drinkers with tales of her exploits, fly-fishing, drop nets, her gift for the gab, her ruse, ancient and refined, and her tinkerings with net and lead that were no less so; her flesh wandered far afield with a pouch over one shoulder, stuffed with little fish, corn Gitanes, bait; she would stop and plant herself facing the river and whip the somber water with bright nylon, with nickel-plated flies; Hélène's flesh had borne the finest fisherman in the district, perhaps the region. She was Jean the Fisherman's mother and this now sufficed, he would still be there—on his heels near the water's edge watching, grumbling, rejoicing, striking fish, brutally unveiling the mother-of-pearl scales beneath the living light—while she was becoming pulp beneath the earth of Castelnau, next to the church. She spoke to me a little, looked out at me with shrewd eyes and pretended to listen, she knew, of course—although she didn't know that my desires were called Yvonne and they sold me Marlboros. So for a moment I saw both of them there, the one who wandered away and the one who lingered, the callipygian and the soothsayer, each immemorial in her own way. I left the blood red room, the cave with its mothers, its sons, its companions in tractors whom libations make brothers, and its great callipygian molested up above, strutting her stuff, giving this comedy the weight of tragedy, without limits and invisible. The fathers hunt far off in some elsewhere beyond imagining. I went to bed; moonlight entered my room and far off in the lost clearings caressed flints no one saw, a more furious rain burying them. Doors slammed in the black night; the hooded sexes of dogs quivered, they howled. I fell to sleep atop women who push these doors, entering the fields. Jean the Fisherman caught a carp.

And in the morning there was school, the ring of little feet. They learned penmanship while crying, grammar and spelling, all without knowing—and anyway we never know in advance that the little braids are destined to become black as ravens, that long pants will be worn even in the middle of summer—that the world becomes just words and their effects, heavy machinery, job offers, souped-up motorbikes and hunting rifles, parties and movies at the theater in Périgueux; they aren't yet aware that's all there will be between you and what grows from your gut, or, for the little braids, between you and what grows into your gut, pushing upward. The little feet were moving, the big, round eyes looked at me. The knees applied themselves beneath the tables, the hands wrote. The calligraphers from the Third Republic and their fine hands aged on in back while other hands, fervent and precise as well, which patiently cut Acheulean flounder, scale after scale, hone harpoons for fishing, write on water; and I who went on; I, serious as some socialist savant, who taught them spelling in his high collar, his embuttonage with its exuberant ties, his frills and flounces, his brooch, but who, when they had barely reached the courtyard under the rain, stripped and parted a woman of perfect whiteness who sold them lollipops and who smiled at them, who was mother of one of them. Yes, something in my class resembled her, it had bright eyes under plump eyelids and inky hair—but not the breasts or the ass, without even mentioning the earrings, and who therefore didn't resemble her at all: Bernard, her son, who was seven years old and whose flesh was entirely superfluous to hers, because hers was a flesh more impetuous and dense than these thirty little-boy kilos. So there was another form of mediation between us than just the cigarettes and the fabulous stupors that the woods where she appeared induced in me, another currency than these botched encounters, furious and courtly; it was this child.

November came and the rain didn't cease. The Beune was fat, was drowning the fishermen's paths. While we were in the courtyard, cranes flew low in the sky, our faces tipped back, running with water, pondering these great shapes that threw cries onto the dense whiteness of the clouds, slowly raking the sky like a net drawn through the Beune; a farmer killed one, ancient and exhausted, that had come to rest near the water and that I saw at night chez Hélène, on the counter between frothy glasses of beer. The wound was invisible; the white neck hung over this side of the counter, the beak stretched out as if in flight, its neck hanging down. Men in dripping oilskins thrust their fingers into the feathers, kneading the dead crane. She wasn't stuffed, these people didn't have a taste for such things.

Cranes passed and my students learned their times tables. Around this time I climbed toward my little Golgotha, hoping that Yvonne would be wearing the dress I had seen her in the day before, would be wearing the two combs I liked in her hair that bared her cheeks in such a way that one better saw the delicate plumpness that was revealed when her chin flexed toward her neck. The Tabac was filled with people, men come from the hamlets in their Sunday best to replenish their stores of loose tobacco; and the village gossips come from Mass to glean whom they should damn or perhaps spare. Behind all of these stiff-suited shoulders, these flannelette dresses, Yvonne served, as lively and open as ever. She was wearing the combs, she was wearing the dress, her face, bigger than ever, dispossessed me immediately, filled me with unspeakable happiness. A man appeared, who cavalierly swept past everyone and, leaning on the counter, bent lightly toward Yvonne; he spoke a few words that I was too far away to hear, and anyway it seemed to me that he was speaking in a low voice. Below the clean lines of the back of his hair, I noticed a not-very-well-cut suit that hung well on his sloping shoulders nonetheless, and on either side of him his delicate hands resting on the big plastic shelf where the lighters were displayed below. Yvonne looked at him. In an instant, in a blink of an eye, she, so lively just before, so self-possessed and expansive, had a complete change of face. Change? It wasn't that she closed herself off, that she no longer appeared charitable; now she was generating something completely different. Like Jean-Gabriel, perhaps, seeing that ineffable Hand behind the one that drew taut the bow, blessing them both, trembling; but it never occurred to me to think about Jean-Gabriel. She had flushed an even crimson, her white chin hesitating, weighing whether it would continue to bear her smile. It did; but in her eyes was a sort of call, a dream, a refusal sometimes seen on women, on both those of the shadows and of the Mass, a delicious servility and a vain shudder of revolt that was yet more delicious. She bridled, she relented, she offered up both her revolt and her defeat, the two grinding against each other with neither of them prevailing. This occurred in an instant, the man's inaudible murmur, his hands resting on the display case of lighters, Yvonne's vacillating look and this pathos smoldering in her cheeks, the brief burst of the faltering beast, subdued. The man turned around, he was of average height, well built but that was all, with thick, dull blond hair and a low hairline, cheerful little eyes, a large mouth, generous or greedy; he had a ruddy complexion and, as I already said, delicate hands. He hadn't said good-bye, but there was neither coarseness nor hostility in his bearing; instead, a sort of courtesy, like a sort of calm, that reigned over this droopy strongman, this low sort of elegance, his big, straightforward features that had an unexpected charm and him, this charm, this, well. Underneath it was the sort of half-drunken contentment that hunters have after a good shot. The rain fell onto his shoulders, in no particular hurry he made for an old Peugeot that he'd left with its motor running. During the instant of silence that weighed upon the store, I thought about the sound of the blood that was beating in Yvonne's cheeks. The gossips looked at each other with little smiles, the cruelty of which nearly made them seem pretty; the farmers asked for their cigarettes in voices that were heavily tender, but laced with something wrong. As unquestionably was mine. Yvonne lowered her head, bared her cheeks. Selling me my Marlboros, she raised her eyes violently and looked at me as she never had before.

THREE

At the end of November, the weather changed, the waters froze. The flooded fields froze, tufts of bulrush stood frozen over the region. It was the time of year when vehicle registrations were renewed; it was around three, a Sunday. Snow had fallen during the night, these little flakes, dense and reticent, that one sees only in the coldest periods and that don't accumulate very much. It froze solid, the sky was rigid, pure. The light seemed green; another hour of daylight remained. The Tabac was full of unhappy customers waiting impatiently, tapping the toes of their shoes; they grew tired of waiting and left: Yvonne wasn't there; little Bernard was watching the store as he often did, but while he could sell newspapers and cigarettes, he was ignorant of the complicated maneuvers necessary to dispense the tags. I left the store into a gust of wind: I don't know what came over me as I lumbered down la route des Martres; beneath the pungent walnuts, I had to keep myself from running: the pure cold was biting into me, the world was a frozen stocking, a fabulous surface beneath which beat, and I knew not where, a boiling flesh that I felt compelled to seize, that would make me burn; I wanted to peel it back and hear it crackle. My ears were buzzing, I was out of myself. Just out of town is a long straight stretch surrounded by wide fields, beyond the walnuts but not quite to the forest; I stared into these fields as if eye to eye with them, peering to their borders with the trees and back again, all the places where a thousand times Yvonne had manifested in her stockings, all white, her hips naked in the cold, bitten, thrown far from the forest for the benefit of winter and my soul. This big game a thousand times lost. Far in the distance I suddenly saw a few specks coming out of the underbrush that were making their way to the edge of a meadow; as they moved closer, I was able to see the red stain of a hat that danced gently around the uneven terrain; and around the red hat were others, in ponchos, arms that moved brazenly, four or five skimpy lads proceeding with resolve, like little old dwarves. The dwarves were carrying something; they followed their path the length of the field toward the main road without straying from the browned lip of frozen trees. Sometimes Yvonne would take the high road through the fields while on her enigmatic outings; and the dwarves doubtless were there to announce their queen, were dancing around her: and without giving it any further thought, I stepped over the fence and made my way toward them.

They were children from school, those who lived in the Martres commune; so it was I recognized them from far away. What two of them were carrying on a pole resting on their shoulders surprised me greatly, and at first I didn't believe it; but no, it was indeed a fox, suspended by its paws in the old or barbaric manner, and I had no idea why they were taking this thing that way through the cold. Apparently, the animal was dead, the big, abandoned tuft of its tail hung down to the feet of the children, heavily red beneath the green sky. I hurried toward them. This trophy from another age that these little hunters were carrying toward me—the offering they were making me, this fine carnivore borne by backcountry tykes, the bright red bonnet, the ponchos from an earlier age, the clodding bustle of those who were carrying and the drunken dances of the others who were gamboling around them—all this inflated my wickedness, cracked it, honed it with the uneasiness that gives it meaning. I was in an obscene fable. An invisible hatchet swung mightily and shook a tree nearby. The woods filled with the woeful cries of wolves gorging themselves on beautiful victims dear to you; the pole across their shoulders seemed suited for other prey: in place of the red fox, I thought I saw bound there—in icy stockings pushed up by the odd position, all black and raw, foaming—the thick haunches of this bitch. I ran outright, with reason; bulrushes cracked beneath my feet; the air in my ears deafened me; exiting the woods via a little footpath, straight ahead and perhaps terrifying like Constable Ysengrin, and as fierce as his she-wolf—there she stood, just a few feet from me. I could easily have collided with her. I stopped short.

There wasn't a breath of wind along the edge of the woods. She was in her Sunday best, in one of those ample brown car coats that one imagines draped from the shoulders of haughty young ladies from the turn of the century who, with a little finger raised skyward and a cherry red mouth, look through a lorgnette at jockeys weighing in; underneath she wore pearls that despite winter she left bare at her neck; earrings, as always, and fine icy stockings beneath which a tormented whiteness had begun to blush pink in the cold. All this chic at the edge of a lost wood was as out of place as a pornographic doodle on a jockey's pristine shirt. I tried in vain to catch my breath, what cut it short now came from below, sharp as a razor. I believe that she had run as well, her heavy breaths sweeping through her throat, her car coat, her pearls; the scene shook; moreover, the frost revealed these brief breaths, spoke of her willingness or her upset. The cold had slapped her in the face, her lips were raw, chafed, but lipstick covered the gash. She watched the children approach and turned away as if she hadn't seen me: this bit of coquetry moved me more than if she had been naked. Her breaths ceased; she turned toward me slowly, and with a look of rapture more moving than her earrings or the raven diadem or the bursting mouth, her eyes bored into me from a face that floated as if lost at sea, her boiling cheekbones, her steady stare; her nostrils flared; she turned her head a little to the left as if to look toward the woods, but with an affected slowness and without breaking eye contact: and so I saw her right side, and there—highlighting her beauty spot and holding her right cheek in view, budding amply on her neck, flowering lower beneath the car coat and grazing her cheek with this abject petal—was the thick mark, bloated with black blood and more bruised than a black eye, more devoured than her lips—a mark left radiantly by the tail of a whip.

The fire that this vision made circulate through my veins should have made me cry out. Nothing could have equaled the unveiling of this face upon which suddenly had leaped something like her other lips, like the strawberries of her breasts. Her glorious face bore into mine, and as I held onto it she reddened ceaselessly. Arrogance and shame fought for that face, like a piece of meat between two dogs; and like a piece of meat, she resisted. The children were upon us; would she lift up her dress right there and reveal the rest, in front of them? She was drunk. They were upon us, they passed, with loud, boisterous hellos; the dwarves that brought me stones looked at the queen with round frank eyes, the tobacconist; one of them carried a little basket filled with white eggs; the fox swung at the rhythm of their steps, its mouth open upon and full of little bones set in black gums; the stiff tail was frozen. I saw this in a flash, our eyes did not leave each other. The she-wolf hadn't looked at anything. "What is it?" I said, out of myself. I don't know what I was talking about, what unsayable red or crimson trophy I meant, but these words were strangling me, they had to get out: I still heard them whistling in the frozen air, fogging the mirroring metal of the hatchets echoing around us. I was a tree. "They are carrying it," she said, "to the houses, to show it off. People give them a little money, eggs. At night they'll skin it against a door." Her voice was too sharp and lashing, with a sort of precocity that made it crack; she curled her lips and lisped a little. By now her face was well beyond red and her words were pure shame, like the fresh mark that burned in the cold. "What do they do with the body?" I continued with the same elation. She hesitated, her sharp voice springing forward and breaking off cleanly, her mouth dry; and in one breath, she at last lowered her eyes and said: "I suppose that they give it to the dogs." The piece of meat ripped apart, her hands stiffened in the pockets of her coat, she shuddered. Her chin was trembling.

And once again she was the woman who sold Marlboros to the young instructor and made the best of things in Castelnau. She existed. The callipygian Venus was only a woman. She turned away as one does when one is about to cry and without a word left me there in the field and moved toward the village where she would sell tags, one of her own on her cheek. She had another one on the fat of her calf; it looked astonishing beneath the black nylon. She walked slowly, immoderately. She swayed as she walked. The little hoods were disappearing beneath the walnuts. At their shoulders in the shadows, the emblematic animal—the coyote or the dingo, the fox, the cunning trickster of old cosmogonies, red and sly, the fabulist's flatterer—had long since been invisible, and was doubtless swaying too. Night was falling, the sharpening stars pinned themselves on high. The hatchets struck dully at my back, echoing around me. A tree collapsed in a crash of barn doors opened and closed by the wind. Lights came on in Castelnau. Still along the great night a pure white hand held out in the west. The queen was at the bottom of the field, high-heeled like a crane, naked beneath her furbelows, like a scaled fish. Her hips were moving. I thought about what had made them move even more a little while ago. I thought about her vivacity, her cruel elegance; the arrogance of beauty; the shame that crushed her high-pitched voice; the sound of her cry. I tried to imagine her as Bernard's mother. The dry bulrushes caressed her ankles, ran her stockings, cut. I felt this in my stomach. Beneath the shadows, beneath the coat, beneath the skirt, beneath the nylons, the earrings, the pearls and the Sunday best, beneath Milady's braids and gathers, hugging the dark stockings, lay this dazzling daylit flesh where at its whitest I imagined, twenty times over, beaten, received during intense thrusts and punctuated by sobs, the heavy, unanswerable phrase that remained forever redundant, forever jubilant, suffocating, black, the absolute authorship she wore on her face.

FOUR

That night I learned of an old custom, surely long since abandoned, that held if a hunter were to kill a fox, he should entrust the pelt to innocents, so they might walk from village to village and rejoice in the ostentatious defeat of this pest while earning some coin off its skin: the animal, they said, carries rabies. Long ago it was said that it stole eels, hunted down she-wolves, and devastated vineyards. I always relate it to Yvonne's defeated and devastated flesh, to her soul that had been flayed one deep cold night.

I should mention that I had a girlfriend in Périgueux. She was a student there and came to visit me in her little old Renault, often on the spur of the moment as her schedule allowed. She adored Hélène and I think the feeling was shared: sometime they would spend all day in the kitchen of the auberge while I was at school, or at a table in the main room where Madelaine, or Mado—that was what I called her—drank from the same cup of coffee that had long turned cold, and during the course of her daydream made circles with her cup on the polished wood, bringing Hélène's wrath down upon her. They talked and exchanged recipes for jam, passed photos, and showed off pieces of their wardrobe; Mado complaisantly sang the praises of her stockings and then displayed them; occasionally, she looked upset when I returned from class, the old woman was dreamily easygoing, perhaps more elegantly so than usual, her gray forelock tucked under her scarf; they had talked about men, about what made Jean the Fisherman hunt for eels, about the late innkeeper who was as good as any other when she'd had something under those pretty old clothes and he'd had hands to remove them, about me, always evasive, touching her lightly, almost caressing, but pushing away at every turn, toward the Beune below, toward the fox above, the fiery weight that crushed us, me, the innkeeper, Jean, and the others. These back-kitchen councils gave me a feeling men have from time to time: irritation mixed with a vague fatuity prompted by the sudden certainty that knives were being sharpened in preparation for one's return. They smiled at me, made me coffee, cut me big slices of cake. All of this was too clear; I took refuge in some corner with my papers to grade, while I listened to this complicated jumble coming from my Wallachian drinkers darkening into their beers, seeing something in the black and trying hard to talk about it, the ghost of Jean the Fisherman scrutinizing the deep black outdoors, poaching, looking for meaning in every puddle of the great bayou where we were. I waited for all this to end, these stories of nets and stockings: the council eventually tired of brushing gently against the unspeakable; Mado suddenly noticed I was there; we left. We took the old Renault, stopping along a sunken lane, and I seized her roughly across the stick shift, in this little toy car that in this instance seemed more like a prison. She was more turned on by her conversations with Hélène than by my maneuvers: I didn't say a word, did her with my eyes closed, without preamble, giving everything to Yvonne, into her smooth hand that bore my cigarettes, onto the distant gathers of her Sunday best, all along the black gash a scarf had hidden for a fortnight. Mado was easy, she made the best of it, as most do, I suppose. She was a brunette too, thinner, Mediterranean, as they say. In the Renault, she made little cries like a mouse, as when one enjoys a meal. The excessive preparations and the total defeat, the leaps and the tears, the great hatchet at the tiny conjunction of two sexes, love, in a word, wasn't her thing. I should say that I wasn't of very much help, I had this elsewhere: on the square hung a consecrated blade.

We would take walks, visit the surrounding area, from Font-de-Gaume to Lascaux, from La Ferrassie to Sous-Grand-Lac. Yes, of course: beneath these places run rivers, cutting holes through the limestone. Above these holes, reindeer made for summer pastures endlessly, climbing from the Atlantic in spring to the green grass of l'Auvergne surrounded by their thundering hooves, an immense dust cloud on the horizon, their antlers above, and the doleful head of one pushing into the rump of the next; and there, in the dissolute gully that cradles and nurses the Vézère, the two Beunes, and the Auvézère, we waited for them with *Dabs, Parrot's Beaks,* and cries; and the lichen eaters heard the drums in the distance, saw the fires as if night and day were watching the smoke, but made for the drums without deviation, stretching out in the narrows beside the water, trembling; they plowed straight ahead; because if the reindeer had been able to conceive of a god or a devil, they would have prayed and pondered, then and there, seasonal and unstoppable, each April burgeoning suddenly everywhere like the horns piercing their brows, unleashed without reason like gods, manifesting in a single body endlessly multiplied and animated by a single will that drives them mad, in noisy hordes, men carrying hatchets, graves filled with pikes; and they would have thought that this god was clement, because after all only a part of them was truly present, and remained there all summer enjoying the golden lichens on the basalt, the sun that sets behind the gently sloping round volcanoes when the weather is beautiful and the day is spent ruminating grass. And the men who were the gods of these reindeer, after eight days of charivari, of blood, of live forces in the narrows, skinning, salting, din, these early days of April that allow them to do nothing for the rest of the year, to watch, to talk, filling their bellies, enjoying their wives and loving the little babies that spring forth, these men, and it seems that it's true since the carbon 14 dated it all conclusively as if decreed by some socialist savant, when they'd had enough of their children and their women, of the interminable discussions in a blood red hut with their great hats rung with antlers and feathers, men descended into the caves and made paintings. Not all the men: only those with more delicate hands, a more ready or tortuous spirit, single hearts that went at night to look for meaning in the puddles of the Beune, and not finding it there gathered at a place of opaque stones that have meaning, words and combinations of stones and words that make sense, and out of these combinations, strength; those who wished to expiate the blood of the deer, but not for the beautiful eyes of the deer, rather, to be free of every care and to kill better the next year and without remorse, with a hand that nothing would still; those who were afraid of the dead spoke to them better than anyone, with a little paper or not, a tricolor scarf or not; those to whom the mayor of some little spot in the Dordogne, perhaps Eyzies, speaks without knowing it, that in his kiss he joins and welcomes beneath the eyes of the citizens whose hats are in their hands, on the eleventh of November, with his crib before a monument to the dead. The mayor of Les Eyzies perhaps thinks of them during the ringing of the bells for the dead. And it once was not uncommon to take these few to be shamans, to be as knowledgeable as socialist savants and as pious as Mohicans, calling forth wild game and rain while drawing them in the dark, then dancing before this imposing display where great cows jump, or one lone wolf runs; and it is now not uncommon to see these men as artists, as art has become fashionable; the times have tossed the socialist savants and their gesticulating primates to the nettles, as if that were so different, as if the arts too didn't dance in front of the display and shake its doors open to share in its marvels. But upon reflection these were indeed artists, since they made this hole off-limits to others, where they came and entered gingerly and with an air of great mystery, antlers on their heads while they muttered paternosters, and also because they doubtless wrote *Oedipus Rex* and *Theogony* on those walls in a writing made of animals that we can't read. So I distracted myself there from Yvonne, or perhaps went to see her by taking a detour, the long road, as the old bachelors had: we visited these caves behind their hallways, their ticket windows, their uniformed employees, Mado and I; and a hundred times between two submerged lanes between Les Eyzies and Montignac, I repeated this Paleolithic lecture to myself and I repeated it to her.

Once, during Christmas vacation, we were coming back from one of these trips. Between les Martres and Castelnau, coming from les Martres, the road briefly follows the valley before drawing back and taking a detour toward this place I've already mentioned, where there are walnuts, and the hallucinogenic fields that carried Yvonne. At the point where the road veers away from the Beune but is still close to it, you see a dirt road marked by a sign from the local administration: Prehistoric Cave of Chez-Quéret. We had already seen this sign, but the airplanes had overlooked it, the cave not appearing in the guidebooks that direct one's choices. The afternoon had barely begun, the old Renault had already served its amorous office, we had left early in the morning. The road drew us onward. We committed ourselves to it.

It had started to rain again after the eight days of miraculous cold that had delivered Yvonne, whipped. The byroad collapsed into a bog, we bounced around, our wipers beat back and forth. We were above the cliff, the road descended a bit farther; halfway down, there was a house, a barn, a few outbuildings, a field that seemed enormous to me in the black rain. We were at a lower elevation than chez Hélène, but on the same lip of the cliff; the site, the escarpment, the bare limestone were all identical. The high waters of the Beune rose nearly to the road as she widened before the house, flooding the road below; she was muddy, in a hurry, devouring the remains of icicles hanging down all along her banks, like bits of old rags left there through the bitter cold; the bare trees were dripping before us, lamentable like the famous little mammoth of Pech-Merle, which is hairy and dripping, on the thirty-ninth day of the Flood. The scene was sweetly sinister. Mado's sage duffel coat and jeans leaping animatedly from the car warmed my heart, made me laugh. There was a sort of curate's garden to cross; we knocked; someone shouted for us to come in. In the big kitchen floated an acrid odor of dust, immemorial and fossilate, of mud so ancient it had become edible, the smell of cooking beets. Jean the Fisherman, a knife in his hand, was making a soup. From his pouch, a shoulder bag open on the table next to the peppers, protruded an open pack of corn Gitanes.

We wanted to go in. He told us that he didn't deal with the cave, that Jeanjean wasn't around but that he should be back soon, and so he had us sit down. I knew that the fish he sold to restaurateurs throughout the region weren't enough to live on: Jean the Fisherman worked for a farmer from the village of Martres, Jean Lavillatte, who ever since he was a young boy had been called Jeanjean, and who was still called that even though he had grown up, perhaps to distinguish him from the Fisherman with whom people confused him. But if this nickname was familiar to me, rolled like a fat smooth pebble in the mouths of the drinkers chez Hélène between remarks about fishing or threshing machines, I hadn't met the man. So it was there, chez Jeanjean.

Jean the Fisherman asked after news about his mother, to say something, I suppose, and Mado joined in soon enough. She had lit a corn Gitane to make herself seem more at ease, more blue-collar, smoking with great seriousness, her legs crossed and a hand in the pocket of her open duffel coat. She was pretty, natural in this role of conversationalist that seems to bloom in women when their breasts grow, diligent in their pursuit of its mastery like my students are at their times tables. Her feet were moving, hers too. She looked bravely at Jean the Fisherman. But his good will slipped a bit: he didn't stop smiling, beneath this shower of words he continued to build his soup and his stare didn't waver from the potatoes his knife bit into; the fine pointed profile remained in shadow; he responded perfunctorily and had the air of someone who didn't give a damn. He had an air of embarrassment that seemed out of place on him, so delicate, so animated, so playful: he was bothered perhaps that he wasn't far away from here, leaning over the Beune, at night; bothered that we had surprised him during his domestic duties; anguished above all that a young girl was talking to him about his mother as though she knew her better than he, and she did know her better than he, since they were women. He was almost under the eyes of his mother, and his mother was eighteen. He knew this old sweet song, of course, irresistible as it was, and could do little else but focus on his potatoes and smile. He disappeared into this smile, he walked along the river: perhaps he would have preferred to disappear, would rather have been myth than man, pure absence, a glorious apparition always regretted and praised in the mouths of drinkers, like some memory of a day fly-fishing that was only a dream, with trout this big. But he was there: upstream toward Saint-Amand where the two Beunes flow, Jean the Fisherman was fishing, whipping the water and grabbing the scales, but farther downstream he drudged like the others near les Martres, even here on Jeanjean's farm.

The rain threw itself against the windowpane. It was three according to the grandfather clock. In Castelnau, Yvonne, who didn't talk to men about their mothers, who didn't talk about anything because maybe what weighs on men's stomachs weighed on her voice, who therefore talked to them about everything and nothing, Yvonne had just appeared from the waist up behind her counter, her invisible skirt caressing her thighs. She smiled at the buyers of loose tobacco. Boatmen on the Beune rowed toward her; behind they brought a whole team, heads leaned forward beneath great streaming hats, with sharpened blades beneath their coats. I was relaxing into the sweet earthy odor of the beets, I was thinking about her, about the somber appetites of the boatmen. I had stopped listening to Mado babble; steam was lifting the lid of the casserole, Jean the Fisherman was having at the peppers. The door opened, a man entered dripping, wearing a big fur-lined jacket, a balaclava, Wallachian. He freed himself of his gear and appeared: I knew him, I recognized his low sort of elegance, his gentle, slender hand that glided his hat from his head. It was the man with the Peugeot who had made Yvonne blush. My dream had taken flesh, it aligned itself with the series of events that one believed to be real; I had before me this blush, this pathos that had bitten her cheeks. Yvonne's blood beat briefly within my own. I almost saw her there in her stockings. She was behind me, the oven at her hips and steam at her mouth, boatmen holding her roughly. Jeanjean was all over us, pleasant, stocky; he shook our hands like we were old friends, the eager smile, happy; he was extraordinarily at ease, trafficking in this ease, drunk from it, holding forth with this somewhat drunken contentment that never left him. It wasn't that he was full of himself, that there was a trace of self-importance about him, some maneuver by which he tried to get the best of others with this drunkenness; it seemed instead that he would more happily share it: but what did make him happy and danced in his eye was out of reach, was beyond him, detached, as though he were still fishing the Beune even as he spoke with us here. Underneath he seemed calm. It was contagious, Jean the Fisherman's white teeth flashed in an unembarrassed smile. Jeanjean washed his hands, leaning before a little mirror on the sink, smoothing down his thick dark hair with his fingertips, with the same tense satisfaction. He must have been about fifty, but his vigorous drunkenness made him seem younger. He took a pocket lamp and led us outside without his coat; he ran through the rain and entered the barn. He had told us: the entrance to the cave was at the back.

FIVE

In the barn, filling the space with its incomprehensible gears, was a green John Deere combine harvester. We skirted around the machine, worming our way along the length of the wall. There was no wall at the back, it was built onto the cliff. The entrance to the cave was shorter than an average man, about Mado's height: we went in behind Jeanjean. It was as it always is when you walk into these antechambers and you don't know if you'll fall upon a nave of pictures, triumphant cows, or frightened wolves, a vague painted hand, or nothing; neither more nor less so; we followed the circle of his flashlight that he directed where we stepped. We climbed and descended between crumbled stones, we wormed through the fault, we trampled through sinkholes where stones slept, we couldn't make sense of anything. We were afraid of bumping our heads. Everything brimmed with water, the pale soaked clay stuck to our soles, the rains of this sodden winter dripped from above, rivering down in a thousand places; I thought about the floods of fifty centuries that had streamed within, when the glaciers were wreaking their havoc. It was warmer here than on the surface: this hot breath added to the discomfort of being beneath the dead, as if an animal hanging from the vault were breathing on you, crawling comfortably over the ruined sands, always a step ahead of you, just beyond the flashlight's beam but over his shoulder and turning his muzzle toward you and waiting for you at the tunnel's fork, a great, ambulatory abstraction, chaotic and ready to manifest in the low lamplight, something more piercing than Anubis, more powerful than a bull, the universal miasma with the head of a dead sheep, with the teeth of a wolf, straight ahead and upon you in the shadows and watching you. The passageway was long, punctuated by chimneys, small rooms; Jeanjean would stop in these for an instant, walk his beam around the walls, say a few words, geology and anecdote, but he was eager to go farther. We saw no traces of human habitation. I sensed that Mado was somewhat upset, she was clutching my arm and stumbling; at the top of a dry, steep, sandy path where she began to tire, Jeanjean opened a small, waterproof case on the wall, illuminating an electric meter; he threw the circuit breaker. An enormous room illuminated brightly.

It was extraordinary. It was bare. It was the cupola of

Lascaux at the very moment when the old bachelors had entered it, antlers on their heads, and in the torchlight their hearts had leapt in their chests; when the impeccable expanse of white limestone had been unveiled for them alone, creamy, smooth, lightly grained but a grain that all the same they skimmed over with the tips of their fingers, this grainy, milky world, this *mondmilch,* overflowing with candor, this great drapery, served to them as if on an easel between a fringe of dark quartzite and a bulbous ceiling, heavy and secret. The trickster who leads you into the black doesn't always deceive, the universal miasma has its good points, between two gullies, two joints in the rock where they break the bones. There were no paintings. It was Lascaux at the instant when the crouching bachelors wedded their idea, conceived it, breaking the ochre sticks and stirring the wood coals in a puddle, silently, settling the antlered hats next to them; and perhaps they then picked them up and turned them in their hands, their hats, they looked at them sweetly and thought of their earliest childhoods, thought seriously that one day they would have to die, that they loved women and eating, fooling around with antlers on their heads; the clement and insatiable gods looked at them in that moment, breathed through their mouths, felt their joy, and soon threw them to the walls with that joy, standing, uncertain of will but sure of hand, tracing huge red cows more wounded than women but who leaped like them, joyous, hunted. The old bachelors weren't even there, just Jeanjean. He had stopped inside, perfectly visible under the floodlights. He wasn't saying anything, pleased with himself, standing in the heart of this daughter of the floods, vibrant against its immutable whiteness. My desire was situated just so, in Yvonne. In the lamplight, his dull, coarse hair shone brightly; his big greenish wool sweater, glowing as well, hung heavily on his sloping shoulders, his low hands. With one great, slow, somewhat theatrical gesture, his hand rising above him, he embraced the space: "As you can see," he said, "there's nothing here." Despite his smile he was perfectly serious, a bit stiff, and his drunken eyes roamed the walls, avidly, tenderly. Mado, who was leaning on the limestone, gathered her duffel coat close around her, curling into it, watched with her mouth open, dumbfounded. Overcome with his customary enthusiasm, he turned his back on us suddenly and walked to the rear of the gallery, where it opened up into another that sloped downward; he added, as if for himself: "Absolutely nothing." He was already into the next gallery. Mado was giggling.

In the other rooms, diverticula and shafts, illuminated too but not as brightly, there were no human traces: only a few scratches from bears, the whitest marks in the limestone, and, in little low displays carefully arranged that no doubt served as a warning and justified the sign from the tourist bureau, a fair number of fossil bones, metatarsi or vertebrae, which Jeanjean told us were from bears, from foxes and wolves, one of these crepuscular runaways that our ancestors were in the habit of depicting alone in the background, and which the prehistorians call *the third animal* because he turns his back upon these massive, redundant dances, where bison and horses entwine in pairs, mammoth and oxen. Jeanjean was still joyous, benevolent; he told us how he had discovered these bones; Mado laughed openly, not because she was making fun of him, but because this solemnity, these little lights lit for nothing beneath the earth, the excited explanations by our guide and the time we were wasting flabbergasted her, like a practical joke that she was taking well: a little later in the car she would tell me that Jeanjean was full of hot air. But she was tickled too, she was seduced. He had looked at her and spoken to her more than to me, almost with complicity. Past the displays ran a stream that pooled into a vast, handsome green pond; it flowed into the Beune. Jeanjean explained that when he had cleared this part, he had found pure white carps in the pools, white and blind, albino fish spawning for millennia in the black, eyes wide open and white; the electricity had killed them. Mado was dreaming, her eyes on the pond. We reached the expected cul-de-sac and some impassable passageways leading from it, that was all. Jeanjean came back, silent, Mado was dragging. He crossed the white bubble like an arrow; then the narrows, the entryways, and at last the last bottleneck, between the John Deere and the wall. It was raining less. The gray rising sky seemed larger; a hirsute pony ruminated all alone in a field like a little Tartar horse abandoned in the Wallachian landscape; he was trembling. The poor animal pissed, solitary as winter. I saw a steeple between some fir trees, less than a mile away. It was the church in Castelnau. I was shocked; Jeanjean told me that essentially we were right around the corner, that we shouldn't trust the road whose detour distorts distance, that there were a thousand ways through the woods that would take you to Chez-Quéret in under an hour. These geographical caprices seemed to amuse him. He looked toward Castelnau. He was jubilant.

SIX

I have a difficult confession to make: I martyred Bernard. He was a charming child, guileless, wise. His mother—who had him from a failed marriage and had left her acolyte behind, or perhaps the other way around— I believe his mother adored him. She had limitless love for this supernumerary flesh, but as I said, this didn't do him much good. I would see her waiting for him at the gate to the school, perched on her high heels, vigilant, unaffected, surrounded by all the gossips, taller than them all, speaking to them, vivacious, infatuated with nothing, putting a little hat on the boy or holding his shoulder while she talked, then moving off while taking his hand, but what I remember best is of course her smooth hands in the wool hat, her chapped, outlined lips that made her lisp as she cuddled him; I have a disproportionate memory of her departure, her stockinged legs and her hips moving the length of the road where supernumerarily trotted alongside her the well-behaved legs that I can't quite recall. He reached out his arms and took her cheeks in his hands, the enormous earrings, when she bent down to kiss him; the raven hair caressed the child's face, the comb slowly slipping through the mass before tumbling free; and when he walked alongside her, his little schoolbag in one hand, he had his other hand in between the backs of her knees, crumpling and pulling on her skirt, brushing her stockings. In the end, I adored Bernard too. He didn't talk very much, he was curiously reserved for his age: not placid and even less dull, but intensely reflective, as if poised in mid-leap, watching adults with a serious attention that hadn't anything to do with politeness. He looked at you deeply from out of his round eyes, doubtless trying to understand, but the great seriousness and the depth of his zeal gave you the impression that he had understood things before you had, knew what you would do and even forgave you for it. But this was only my impression. Perhaps he had actually understood it all, because there wasn't very much to understand: his Christmas came every day, universal contact with this unplumbable richness, the queenly bearing and the hooker's heels, this piece always bent over him and long since fallen from the sky, these hands that embodied pleasure as the fingertips removed his swaddling clothes, later readying his book bag, his bread and butter, infusing in him a sort of wordless

understanding, dolorous and ecstatic, and so he didn't
need to play very much, to exert himself, he could remain there in his little armchair and look on with something like terror as the milk and honey flowed, fixing the
memory of this outpouring all for him. And he knew in
some way that the source of the milk and honey wasn't
meant for him. He certainly knew this liftable skirt, although it ceased at a certain point even for him, at
boundaries both definite and vague somewhere above
her stockings, where the great gift became a torture one
could neither give nor be given; he knew the outside of
this gift, this refusal, this wardrobe as familiar to him as
the buffet in which was cocoa and cups to have it in, no
more a secret to him than were the contents of Jean the
Fisherman's shoulder bag; he knew the preparations, the
feverish comings and goings in lingerie in front of mir-
rors, heels clattering, and seated in his little armchair he
watched, with his serious stare. He knew her Sunday
best. He watched her tremble beneath it; and he could
doubtless foresee, with the old look of his new eyes, the
burning, the fever that threw her into the night, her raincoat on her shoulders, the night at the heart of which
Jeanjean waited, leaning against his nothing, his limestone Nobody behind the harvester, leaning steadfast,
waiting, suddenly springing through the struts beneath

the blade of moon, he had in his hands the white mask, the night hair, he calmly opened the raincoat and calmly handled her, held her, stripped her to all that milk, her heels twisting and her smooth hands grazing the wall as he took her in a barn. And Bernard, lifting an ear from his little armchair, heard the growling of dogs, he didn't hear the cries of pleasure. But he saw their marks, the chapped lips and the anguished eyes, the dusty heels, and occasionally the more indelible mark, the black honey, the cassis swollen in orgeat, when she came home in the middle of the night with her wet cheeks, when she opened the door to his room a crack, he pretended to wake up, or waking up for real asked her, among silks undone on the ground beneath her feet, what was it, the black honey, and she, telling him that it was nothing, nothing at all, she leaned her face toward him and kissed him full on the lips, crying or laughing. And he went to sleep next to her, clutching this beautiful, victimized body, just as Jeanjean had but in a different way than Jeanjean had, although with no less love, for love varies. He went to sleep and beneath the knife of the moon roosters sang before the fall into the black hole, and a little fox ran through it that he didn't hear because foxes yelp only in dreams. So all that belonged to Bernard, I could see it in his eyes and I know I wasn't wrong. And because of that I would give him bad grades when I felt like it, I had sway over the proceedings, tangentially. The heart of the annoyance, the dolorous debate taking place in my character, was mildly appeased. And without question I was waiting above all for Yvonne to ask me about these injustices, for her to come to see me. But she wasn't one of these mothers who bothers with such conventions, who believes that the future of each of us differs according to our scores on a quiz; her love for Bernard was of a much older variety, she didn't even need to look at my pedantic little marks in red ink, she was from the age of the old bachelors as well: she never came.

I have a very vivid memory. That year at Christmas, Bernard had gotten a bicycle. During the holidays, I had seen him pass and pass again along the steep path in front of *Chez Hélène,* this superfluous flesh pedaling hard, having a hard time of it on the little contraption, his hands still and his elbows raised, amusingly, his head leaned forward seriously. I'm sure that he was going by there just to be seen by me, to show me that Santa Claus had brought him a bicycle, that he had deserved it and therefore he wasn't so bad even though he and the master seemed to be having some sort of misunderstanding; but this bicycle would settle things. He wanted to show himself as worthy of such a fine gift by climbing the steep path with all the force in his little legs; and if at last he saw me out front, out of breath from the steep little climb, he waved to me with a modest little motion that was nonetheless proud, magic, as if to extend to this stubborn master the great generosity of Santa Claus so that he could benefit from it too. But Santa Claus hadn't brought his mother. I turned a deaf ear and barely acknowledged him.

This bicycle annoyed me, as if all my malevolence and guilt had manifested themselves in these three little pieces of aluminum. It pitied me, it was unbearable; and I was disgusted at the thought of Yvonne picking it out in a store in Périgueux, leaving encumbered with this unseemly package like a queen with a shovel at her shoulder. The morning of the first day back, the little one made a desperate move. I had a short stretch of road to cover to reach the school; Bernard, who no doubt had watched for my arrival in the square, passed me on his bicycle, stopped, waited for me, and with his little legs on the ground on one side and the other, pushed the bicycle forward beside me, silently, looking at me out of the corner of his eye with a great deal of introspection, but this time with expectation and fear. I lifted my nose. I was fuming, I had to release this villainy; I deigned to notice him, and without a word about the bicycle, I told him that with his grades he shouldn't be roaming the streets; and that in addition, at this moment he was importuning his master with rudenesses. I moved off with long strides; when I reached the gate, I turned and saw him stopped back along the road where I had left him, his hands on his handlebars and crying without lowering his head, his face one enormous grimace that children make from time to time, naked, as though intent on having the world witness the injustice of the world, calling from their depths to the sky and their mothers. In his hands, the bicycle's chrome shone, as useless as Santa Claus. I could easily have cried myself.

Thus in the classroom, in my office, looking at the case looming above all the industrious lowered heads, among which was Bernard's, in which the iniquitous presence of an unexpected master was veil upon veil hidden by the image of Yvonne in panties getting ready to go, pirouetting on high heels, putting on rouge and rushing to have herself made over in black honey, in this room where the tireless rain ran over the immense windows, I exercised a power that wasn't quite like that of the old bachelors since no great cows hidden in the shadows leapt visibly forth, no lone wolves, but a power that approached something like it as I ceaselessly conceived a great bright shape that would ruthlessly, endlessly weigh upon the world, white and stamped with red like a Marlboro packet, and sunk my wolf's teeth into it. And I also sunk them into the lamb that suckled beneath her. The socialist savants in the case doubtless reproved me because it was their place to do so, because they had worked as youngsters to learn *the roundhand, the slanting roundhand, the roman,* to hide all this, to disguise it beneath enormous paraphs, draped initials, but they absolved me because beneath their little beards they had wolves' teeth as well to dig into fatter necks than were peeking out from children's car coats, thicker thighs beneath crinoline petticoats. For the others, those who had hooked and gutted their flounder, they too condemned me, revering me as they had condemned in secret and revered openly those who scorned the depiction of flounder and instead had made great callipygians under the earth, reigning with this brutal dream. But I couldn't reign over Bernard, not exactly, perhaps because we were alike: doubtless he suffered, but behind this suffering, his miscalculation of the number of superfluous objects—a bicycle, a tyrannical instructor, Jeanjean's harvester, and Jeanjean himself to whom, strangely, his mother would go in her Sunday best, Santa Claus, and his real father too, who toiled in the beyond, which is to say the supermarket in Périgueux, who took him on vacations from time to time—under the weight of incompletion Bernard had in hand an invincible, dolorous plenty, dolorous since for him she ceased at that region above her stockings where she filled herself with something invisible, voluntary, and massive like the God of the catechism, but a plenty he clung to nonetheless, to the backs of her knees, to her full cheeks, to her enormous earrings. And like me, lifting my nose from between two math problems, two paragraphs, Bernard watched this replenishment through the windows, behind the rain that falls to earth and makes room for our dreams, the satiety of our dreams behind this gray curtain where everything is permitted.

The waters rose.

A night came when there was a thick fog, moveless and almost hot, a fog like there had been the night I had arrived. I was eating my cold cuts when Jean the Fisherman came in with his acolytes; their oilskins were dulled as if dulled by breath. Slung across their stomachs were shoulder bags stuffed to bursting. Jean was beaming: he laughed to himself; he surveyed the scene and affected a sort of slowness beneath which his eagerness danced: the drinkers weren't saying a word, they were laughing too, bubbly with impatience as they settled their glasses down gently; they played along with this game that Jean was offering them. At the counter, he calmly undid the straps of the shoulder bag and thrust his hand inside with a gesture that bespoke the silent transgression of some law, a transgression that brought pleasure; he withdrew two or three carp that he hoisted like an Arawak, like a Mohican brandishing by its gills the great Sturgeon one sees only in dreams. The drinkers were unprepared for what he showed them, for these weren't common fish, weren't even mirror carp with their large sparse scales: these were leather carp, scaleless and smooth like water, shimmering and bare. They gleamed and changed in the half-light, under the antique red. The fish collapsed one after another to the counter with flat slaps. The acolytes had them too, though they revealed them more modestly, hoping only to show that they were worthy of their master, as we would expect of vassals. Jean still had a mischievous gleam in his eye, he smiled, he wasn't done yet; he asked the room to guess where he had caught them. Some quickly said near a dam on the Little Beune, toward Saint-Amand, where the leather carp and others sleep far from the live waters they never visit, gleaming invisibly in their darkness, in movelessness, gorging themselves on mud and from it forging a flesh imponderably smooth that barely touches one's tongue. But they hadn't come from there. Not from there, nor far downstream on the smooth stretches of water in Dordogne. Jean looked at the carp for a moment; then, turning his head violently toward us, he said: "I caught them down below. They were coming down the Beune." A report of crocodiles slipping between the bulrushes toward Chez-Quéret wouldn't have shocked us more. It was like some Old Testament marvel. Gudgeons fall in the rain, sturgeons spawn in the Vézère; queens that are carp from their bellies down are surprised in their baths by an ardent man, their tails beat fervently, splashing water into the sky. They flee, crying beneath the blade of the moon. Hélène took them pensively and went to gut them in the sink. She ran the water. She took a moment to reflect, as did Jean; they looked at all the pink hidden in fish, revealed when one opens them. Below, terrified, carp were tumbling in the current, unable to survive, shaken deep within, their white leather torn by stones; through the fog Jean the Fisherman lifted them with one movement, they swelled like wineskins, bursting, greedily, mouths open wide. Boatmen who had dismounted and were crouched in the bulrush watched them leap at last onto the grass to die. They showed us their white teeth. Hélène poured a few drops from a bottle into the sink, a scent stronger than the barrels, than the cigarette butts, this bleach that diffuses the smell of killing. Elsewhere,

Jeanjean was honing this nothing, other carps trembling under his hands, making them rise from the water, reviving them indefinitely in the moss, hoisting them, suffocating, by their gills, and plunging them under again; Yvonne in this bath with her mouth open was singing a hard song, was dying, indefinitely, was saying as much. Jean the Fisherman was drinking a rum, his head nodding gently, the night stronger than he. The oilskins were departing, and suddenly outside the fog drew them in. Hélène's hands on her apron smelled of fish, she watched her son who knew how to catch them: when you have seen the great Sturgeon, you know where to find the others, or so he told you in a dream. Down below, Bernard's eyes were open in the dark to the bright fog. And at last we all were sleeping, while the Beune flowed on.

Pierre Michon was born in Cards, France, in 1945. His first work of fiction was published in 1984, and since that time his reputation as one of the foremost contemporary French writers has become well established. He has won many prizes, including the Prix France Culture for his first novel, *Vies minuscules;* the Prix Louis Guilloux for the French edition of *The Origin of the World;* and the Prix de la Ville de Paris in 1996 for his body of work. He has published nine books and has seen his novels, stories, and essays translated into German, Dutch, and Italian. A tenth book will be published in 2003. He lives in Nantes, France.

Wyatt Alexander Mason's first translation, Pierre Michon's *Masters and Servants,* was a finalist for the French American Foundation prize. His translation of the complete works of Arthur Rimbaud, *Rimbaud Complete,* was published by The Modern Library. He is currently at work on translations of Michon's *Vies minuscules, Rimbaud le fils,* and *Mythologies d'hiver;* Arthur Rimbaud's complete correspondence; and a new edition of Dante's *La Vita Nuova.*

The
Origin of the World
was designed and typeset on
a snowy January day in Adobe
Garamond and Helvetica Neue by
Mr. Mark Barry of sübata, in beautiful
Hoboken, New Jersey, with an illustra-
tion by Mr. Robert Longo. Bound and
printed on acid-free paper by
Sheridan Books, in Chelsea,
Michigan, 2002.

•